W9-DJQ-940

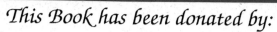

This Book has been donated by:

LITERACY
VOLUNTEERS

of
AMERICA Inc.

487-4444

The Putnam and Grosset Group

We hope that you enjoy it!

Name _____

THE BOY WHO ATE MORE THAN THE GIANT
and Other Swedish Folktales

Retold and illustrated by Ulf Löfgren

Translated from the Swedish by Sheila LaFarge

Collins + World in cooperation with the U.S. Committee for UNICEF

Library of Congress Cataloging in Publication
Data

Main entry under title:
The Boy who ate more than the giant and other
    Swedish folktales.
    (A storycraft book)
CONTENTS: The boy who ate more than the
giant.—The master tailor.—The three billy goats
Bruse.
    1. Tales, Swedish. [1. Folklore—Sweden]
I. Lofgren, Ulf. II. Series.
PZ8.1.B674   398.2'09485   [E]   78-8653
ISBN 0-529-05450-7
ISBN 0-529-05451-5 lib. bdg.

Published by William Collins + World Publishing
Company,
New York and Cleveland, 1978.

LEROY COLLINS
LEON COUNTY PUBLIC LIBRARY
200 W. PARK AVENUE
TALLAHASSEE, FL 32301

Contents

A STORYCRAFT BOOK
Storycraft Books are specially designed to give young people an authentic introduction
to the cultural traditions of other children around the world.

The Boy Who Ate More than the Giant

Once upon a time there was a boy who looked after goats in the woods. One morning he happened to wander all the way to the mountain where a giant lived.

The boy's goats were no different from any others. They made no end of mess and noise wherever they went. They clattered up and down and chomped on leaves and ripped at twigs and gnawed the bark off trees. The little kids bleated, and the big billy goats butted each other so hard that their horns resounded. So there was such a racket and commotion that the giant down in his mountain cottage finally woke up.

He got up and listened. Then he went out to see what it could be. When he saw that a mere goatherd boy had destroyed his sweet morning sleep, he became mightily enraged and wanted to catch the boy and punish him.

But the boy and his goats ran off as fast as

they could. And as the boy ran, he turned over in his mind how he might repay the giant for his nastiness.

In the evening, when he had driven his goats home, he went into the cottage, where he found his mother standing by the stove, making cheese. She had warm milk in the pot and had added rennet, and the curd was just separating from the whey. The boy waited until she took a piece and formed it into a cheese.

"Give me that cheese, Mother dear," he bade her, "so I can take it with me into the forest tomorrow."

"You're welcome to it," replied his mother, handing it to him.

The boy put it in the ashes of the hearth and rolled it back and forth. Soon it looked like a gray stone. His mother was very startled.

"Have you gone mad, my darling?" she said. "You mustn't waste God's gifts like that."

The boy patted her arm.

"Do not be angry, Mother dear," he replied. "I can tell you, this cheese is not wasted. I know just what it will be good for; indeed, I do."

The boy rolled the cheese in the ashes a few more times. Then he put it into his big leather satchel and laid himself down peacefully to sleep.

Next morning he rose early, dressed, and slung the leather satchel on his back. He let out the goats and headed the herd right for the giant's mountain. It didn't take long for the goats to start bleating and bullying, so that the giant woke up.

This time he did not need to wonder what the commotion was. Straightaway he opened the cottage door and strode out, heading for the boy. He looked terribly angry and cruel. The boy felt quite frightened, but he looked the giant straight in the eye.

"Be off with you right now, you wretched mite," yelled the giant, "or I'll squeeze you to bits just as I'm squeezing this stone."

He leaned down and picked up a large gray stone from the ground and crushed it, so that it flew into a thousand fragments.

But the boy did not let himself become terrified. He leaned down and pretended to take up a stone. Instead he swiftly dug his cheese out of his satchel. And this he squeezed, so that the whey ran out between his fingers and dripped on the ground.

"If you," he said, "do not leave me alone, I'll squeeze you so that all that is left of you will be a wet drop, as I'm doing to this stone."

When the giant saw this he turned white with terror and hurried off into the mountain. All that day and all night he hid there wondering about the boy's incredible strength.

But the boy led his herd happily around in the

woods, and when evening came, he ambled home with them. He told his mother the great use he had found for his little gray cheese, and she patted his cheek.

The following morning he rose early, dressed, and let out the goats, heading for the giant's mountain. It didn't take long for the goats to start bleating and bullying, so that the giant woke up.

Now he no longer had to wonder what the commotion was. Straightaway he opened his cottage door.

"Good morning to you, old man," nodded the boy. "Today why don't we match our strengths once more?"

To save face, the giant could not very well say no.

"Wouldn't it be a good test of strength," said the boy, "if one of us could throw your ax so high into the air that it would never fall back down again?"

Yes, the giant couldn't deny that that would be a good show. They should try it right away, and the giant threw first. He swung it with all his might, and the ax sailed high into the sky. But though it traveled high, it soon came down again.

"That was somewhat of a failure," said the boy, "but don't let it depress you, old man. You can try again, and then I'm sure it will go better."

The giant took the ax again and swung it both long and well. When he finally let it go, it sailed so high that it could hardly be seen. A long time passed before the ax hit the ground again.

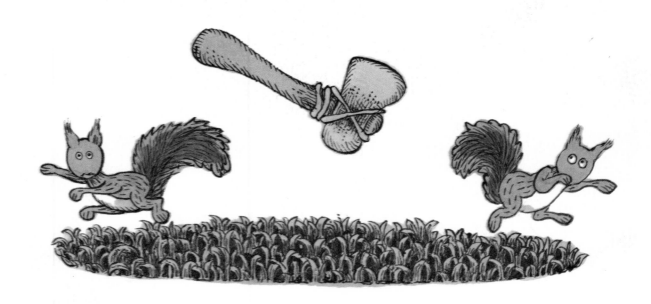

"I would never have thought that you would be so feeble," said the boy. "Wait, now you'll see a real throw. Stand here in front of me and look really hard up into the sky. Because when I throw the ax, you have to be very alert if you want to see it go."

The giant stood dead still, staring up into the sky as hard as he could. The boy took the ax and swung his arm as if he meant to throw the ax very hard. But just as he got the ax with great difficulty over his shoulder, he very deftly let it slip down into the leather satchel that hung on his back.

"Now you've just seen your ax for the last time," said the boy. "I promise that on my honor."

And then the boy sat down on the ground, breathing heavily.

The giant marveled how the ax could have vanished from sight so fast. He stood there a long while, waiting for it to reappear. But though he waited, there was no ax to be seen.

The giant thought to himself that the boy must be terribly strong although he looked so little and frail.

One autumn day the boy was out in the woods when he met the giant once again. The giant thought that such a strong boy was just what he needed for a servant. Then he would soon get as much use out of him as he could. Later something could probably be done when he wanted to get rid of him.

So when they met this time, the giant asked whether the boy would like to work for him.

"Maybe that wouldn't be such a bad idea," said the boy.

"If you go about your work sensibly, I'll give you three bushels of gold," answered the giant. "But if you don't, I have the right to cut three broad strips of skin off your back."

The boy said that he could not complain about a wage like that. He wanted to start working immediately.

They climbed up into the giant's home and there met the giantess. She was as ugly as sin and so abominable that the boy thought she was much worse than the giant himself. All around inside the cottage was the giant's wealth, piles of gold and silver, all of which the giant had stolen from innocent people.

The boy's first task was to follow the giant out into the woods to fell an oak tree. When they came to the oak, the giant asked the boy whether he wanted to hold the tree or to chop.

"I'll hold," replied the boy.

"Well then, hold!" said the giant.

"I am too short," answered the boy.

"That is easily remedied," said the giant.

He bent the trunk to the ground and offered the top of the tree to his servant. The boy grasped it and was supposed to hold it down firmly, but as soon as the giant let go, the oak sprang back up, tossing the boy high into the air. It happened so fast that the giant couldn't follow him with his eyes.

The giant stood still for a long time wondering where his servant had gone. But since no boy could be seen, he took the ax and began to chop. When a good long time had passed, the boy came back. He had been flung very far. The giant asked why he hadn't held on to the oak, but the boy would hear none of that.

"Now I have shown you how far I can jump," he said. "I just wonder whether you, old man, could jump that high."

The giant answered, as the truth would have it, that he didn't believe he could.

"I thought as much," said the boy. "But if I do all the jumping, then it's only fair that you do all the chopping."

That the giant could not refute, and so he chopped down the mighty oak alone. Then the tree had to be carried home.

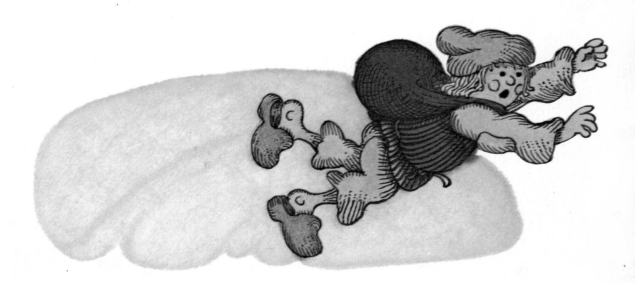

"You'll be old and weak soon," said the boy, "so you should carry the leafy top, and I, being young, will take care of the heavy trunk."

The giant thought this was a handsome offer and immediately lifted the light end of the oak onto his shoulder. But the boy shouted that the tree was on an angle and the giant should shift it forward until it was straight.

The giant shifted and shifted until finally he had the whole trunk balanced on his shoulder. Then the boy hopped up into the tree and hid behind a big branch so that the giant could not see him.

Now the giant thought that the load was really heavy, but consoled himself that the boy carrying the big end must be having a worse time of it. After a while, he moaned heavily with every step he took.

When they finally came to the mountain, the giant was half-dead from the load. He threw the oak on the ground, but before that, the boy had jumped down and now stood smartly at attention beside the thick trunk.

"Aren't you tired yet?" asked the giant.

"Tired?" repeated the boy. "I'll never be tired, you may be sure, if I never have harder work than this. In fact, the oak was not too heavy for one of us to have carried it home all alone."

After that work, the giant had to rest the whole day.

"As soon as day breaks tomorrow, we'll go out

to the barn and start threshing," he told the boy in the evening.

But that the boy did not like.

"No, old man, surely we should get started with our day's work earlier than that," he said.

"If you felt as much like working as I do, we would begin threshing before dawn."

The giant feared that the boy would call him lazy, so he agreed. Then he lay down to sleep and snore.

Early in the morning, while it was still dark, the boy padded over to the giant's bed and shook him until he woke. Then they both walked over to the threshing barn. The giant knew where he kept his two big flails, and he groped his way right to them. One he kept; the other he handed to the boy. The latter tried to lift his flail, but it was so heavy that he couldn't even raise it off the floor. So he left it in a corner and instead took up a big stick that was leaning there.

"Right, now let's begin," he said.

And every time the giant walloped his flail onto the threshing floor, the boy pounded hard with his stick. The giant noticed nothing, and this they kept up until daylight began to peek in between the cracks in the walls.

"Now it must be time for us to go home for breakfast," said the boy.

"Yes," the giant huffed and puffed. "Both of us have done enough to deserve food."

After they had eaten, the giant walked over to the cow barn alone. He intended to fetch his magical oxen to pull his plow across his fields. There was no door to the barn; instead the giant grabbed the building and lifted it. He led the magical oxen out of their stalls and then put the building back on its stone foundation. After work he returned to the boy.

"Now take the dog," he said, "and let him show you the way to the barn. Where he goes in, let the oxen follow him. But if you cannot carry out this job intelligently, I'll take those three strips of flesh off you right away."

The giant looked very crafty when he said that, and the boy realized that now it was a matter of life or death.

When they came to the barn, the dog slipped in through a hole in the stone foundation. Seeing that there was no door, the boy immediately realized what the giant usually did to let the oxen into the barn. He swiftly understood that now there was only one way out, if he wanted to save his skin. He took the ax from his satchel, chopped the magical oxen into pieces and tossed the pieces in through the hole. Then he walked back and asked whether any other urgent tasks needed to be done, because he could do them as well.

"Did you really get the oxen into the barn?" asked the giant.

"Yes, old man," replied the boy. "Of course, it was somewhat difficult getting them in the same hole that your dog used. But when I di-

20

vided them up a little, it went like a breeze."

When the giant heard what had been done, he became completely beside himself with rage. He went to the giantess.

"Listen, old woman," he said, "can't you, with all your clever ideas, think up some way to get rid of him?"

"My advice is to pretend nothing has happened and wait until tonight," replied the giant woman. "When he goes to sleep, you steal up to him with your club, smash him to a pulp, and then you never need fear him again."

But the boy had been standing by the door to the cottage and had heard every single word.

When evening came, he went into the giantess' storeroom and took as large a butter churn as he could lift. This he silently carried to his room, put it in the bed, and spread the fur cover over it. Then he hid behind the door and waited to see what would happen.

Around midnight the giant rose and took his club. He tiptoed up to the boy's bed, raised the club to strike, and brought it down as hard as he could. He heard a tremendous crack and something spurted into his face. Then he felt mightily content and left.

"Ha, ha, ha," he laughed, "I've just smashed that wretch to pieces."

The giantess was very pleased and praised her husband's bravery.

"Now we can sleep peacefully," she said. "We need never fear that sly servant again."

But as soon as they had fallen asleep, the boy took out the pieces of the butter churn and dried up the buttermilk. Then he lay down to rest a while.

It was not yet daybreak when he went in to the giant couple to say good morning to them. They stared at him, not wanting to believe their eyes. The hair rose on the giant's head.

"What? You're still alive?" he shouted. "I was so sure that I killed you with my club last night."

All that day the giant went around thinking to himself that he would be sure to do his job better tonight. No matter how hard he pondered, he couldn't figure out how the boy could have escaped him.

That evening when the giant and his servant were to eat their dinner, the old lady put out porridge for them.

"That's fine," said the boy. "Now we can compete to see which of us can eat the most—you, dear old man, or I."

This the giant agreed to straightaway. At least I can eat, he thought. It would be really extraordinary if I couldn't win this contest.

So they sat down at the table with the porridge bowl between them and each took up a spoon. But the boy was crafty. He had fastened his big leather satchel in front of his stomach and covered it with his shirt. And for each spoonful of porridge he stuck into his mouth, he let seven spoonfuls slip down into the satchel. After the giant had eaten seven bowls of

24

porridge, he was so full that he huffed and puffed and groaned and simply could not eat any more.

But the boy was still shoveling it in as eagerly as ever.

The giant looked at him with astonishment.

"How can it be," he asked, "that you who are so little can eat so much?"

"That I'll be happy to teach you, old man," said the boy. "When I've had enough to eat, I cut a big slit in my stomach and empty out the porridge. Then I can eat just as much again right away. Watch me now!"

He took his knife and slashed the satchel in front of him so that the porridge poured out onto the floor. The giant thought that this was a really good idea. So he immediately took his knife and stuck it straight into his huge stomach. But all that happened was that he fell right down dead on the spot, and when the old lady saw this, she burst apart from fright.

Now the boy was alone in the giant's home. He rinsed his satchel and sewed it up again. Then he put in the three bushels of gold that the giant had promised him if he set about his work diligently. He felt sure that he had earned them. Then he slung his satchel on his back and returned home to his mother. She was more than a little happy, as you can imagine, to have her son back, safe and sound, and a rich young fellow besides.

And that is the end of _that_ story.

The Master Tailor

Once upon a time there was a small gentleman, who went to the tailor with a little piece of cloth which he wanted to have made up.

"Good day to you, master tailor," said he with a bow.

"Good day to you," said the tailor. He was sitting, of course, on the table, as tailors do.

"Could I have a little coat made out of this small piece of cloth?" asked the little gentleman.

"Well, yes," said the tailor.

"When might it be ready?"

"On Saturday."

"That's fine, master tailor. Thank you so much. Good-by now, sir." Then the little gentleman left.

And so the week passed and Saturday came and the little gentleman returned to the tailor.

"Good day to you, master tailor, is my coat ready yet?"

"Alas, no."

"It isn't finished? Why is that?"

"Alas, as it turned out, I couldn't make a coat out of that piece of cloth."

"Couldn't make a coat of it? What *could* you make of it, then?"

"A pair of trousers."

"Oh, a pair of trousers. When will they be ready?"

"On Saturday."

"That's fine, master tailor. Thank you so much, sir. Good-by now, sir." Then the little gentleman left.

And so the week passed and Saturday came and the little gentleman returned to the tailor.

"Good day to you, master tailor, are my trousers ready yet?"

"Alas, no."

"They aren't ready? Why is that?"

"Well, alas, as it turned out, I couldn't make a pair of trousers out of that cloth."

"Is that so? What *could* you make of it, then?"

"A vest."

"Oh really, a vest. When will that be ready?"

"On Saturday."

"That's fine, master tailor. Thank you so

much. Good-by now, sir." Then the little gentleman left.

And so the week passed and Saturday came and the little gentleman returned to the tailor.

"Good day to you, master tailor. Is my vest ready yet?"

"Alas, no."

"It isn't ready? Why is that?"

"Well, alas, as it turned out, I couldn't make a vest of that cloth."

"Indeed, so you couldn't make a vest of it! What *could* you make of it?"

"A pair of gloves."

"Oh, a pair of gloves. When will they be ready?"

"On Saturday."

"That's fine, master tailor. Thank you so much. Good-by, master tailor." Then he left.

And so the week passed and Saturday came and the little gentleman returned to the tailor.

"Good day to you, master tailor, are my gloves ready yet?"

"Alas, no."

"They are not ready? Why is that?"

"Well, alas, as it turned out, I couldn't make a pair of gloves of that cloth."

"Really? Then what *have* you made for me?"

"Why, nothing at all. But it took a great deal of time and work."

"Is that so? A great deal of work to make nothing-at-all? Then it must be fine, master tailor. Thank you so much. Good-by to you, sir."

And so the little gentleman left—with nothing-at-all.

The Three Billy Goats Bruse

Once upon a time there were three billy goats who were going to the upland pasture to fatten themselves on lush, green grass. And the name of all three was Bruse.

On the way to the pasture there was a bridge they had to cross. Under the bridge lived a troll, a really wicked troll, with eyes as big as plates and a nose as long as a broom handle.

First to reach the bridge was the littlest billy goat Bruse.

Clip-clop, clip-clop, clip-clop, went the bridge when he walked on it.

"Who is walking on my bridge?" shrieked the troll.

"It is little billy Bruse. I'm on my way to the pasture to fatten myself up," answered the billy goat in a small, weak voice.

"I'm coming to eat you," said the troll.

"Don't take me, I'm too little, too little. Wait until middle billy Bruse comes. He's much bigger."

"I'll do just that," said the troll.

In a short while middle billy Bruse came to the bridge.

Clip-clop, clip-clop, clip-clop, went the bridge when he walked on it.

"Who is striding across my bridge?" screamed the troll.

"Middle billy Bruse. I'm on my way out to pasture to fatten myself up," said the goat in a firm voice.

"Now, I'm coming to eat you," said the troll.

"No, don't take me, wait for big billy Bruse. He's much, much bigger!"

"That I will," said the troll.

By and by along came big billy Bruse. He was so big and heavy that the bridge creaked and groaned when he walked on it.

CLIP-CLOP! CLIP-CLOP! CLIP-CLOP! it went.

"Who is stomping on my bridge?" yelled the troll.

"THIS IS BIG BILLY BRUSE," roared the billy goat in reply.

"And I'm coming to eat you," said the troll.

"COME RIGHT AHEAD! I HAVE TWO LONG, SHARP HORNS FOR YOU TO FEEL. AND I HAVE STRONG LEGS TO KICK WICKED TROLLS WITH," said the billy goat.

And with that big billy Bruse rushed at the troll, spiked him on his horn, whirled him around through the air in a wide circle, and sent him whizzing off so far that the troll disappeared forever. Then the billy goat ran on up to the meadow where there was so much good grass that the goats grew so fat that they were quite unable to walk home. And if that fat hadn't worn off them, they would surely be up there still.

And clippety, clip-clop, this tale's come to a stop.

ABOUT ULF LÖFGREN

Ulf Löfgren's interest in folklore is of long standing. A graduate of Uppsala University, his fields of study were history of art and history of literature and folklore. He began to illustrate picture books in 1959 after several years of pursuing a career in advertising, and his very first book brought him the Elsa Beskow Award, a greatly acclaimed honor in Sweden. Since then he has won plaques at the Bratislava International Biennale in 1971, 1973, and 1975; and in 1977 he won the Grand Prix there. He has been the chairman of the Swedish Society of Illustrators (1971-1975) and his work is exhibited in the Swedish National Gallery. He also creates television shows for children and has made at least a hundred programs for Swedish Television to date.

He lives with his wife, who is a teacher, and their two children in Lidingö, a small town near Stockholm. In the summertime they vacation on an island in the Baltic Sea where they own a big old house that creaks and groans with age, and keeps them very busy. Besides protecting the house against the ravages of time, Mr. Lofgren's other main hobby is playing the violin.

ABOUT THE STORIES

All three of the stories in this book are favorites of Ulf Löfgren and his family, and are well-known to all children growing up in Sweden. *The Three Billy Goats Bruse* is familiar in other countries as *The Three Billy Goats Gruff.* The story of *The Master Tailor* has a quality of Carrollian nonsense, but in addition it is often quoted in Sweden when someone has put in a great deal of time on a project with little or nothing to show for the effort, somewhat like the mountain that labored and brought forth a mouse. Variants of *The Boy Who Ate More Than the Giant* can be found in many parts of Europe, as far south as Italy, but its oldest form is Scandinavian.